Pig Pig Grows Up

by David McPhail

A Unicorn Book • E. P. Dutton • New York

Library of Congress Cataloging in Publication Data

McPhail, David M Pig Pig grows up.
(A Unicorn Book)

Summary: Only when faced with a dire emergency does Pig Pig finally react like a grown-up and admit he is not a baby anymore.
[1. Babies—Fiction. 2. Pigs—Fiction] I. Title.
PZ7.M2427Pi [E] 80-350 ISBN: 0-525-37027-7

Published in the United States by E. P. Dutton, a Division of Elsevier-Dutton Publishing Company, Inc., New York

Published simultaneously in Canada by Clarke, Irwin & Company Limited, Toronto and Vancouver

Editor: Emilie McLeod Designer: Riki Levinson

Printed in the U.S.A. First Edition
10 9 8 7 6 5 4 3 2 1

Pig Pig was the baby of the family. His brothers and sisters had grown up and left home long ago. But Pig Pig refused to grow up.

He still wore his sleep suit, though it was much too tight, and he continued to sleep in his crib, even though his feet hung over the end.

At breakfast, Pig Pig sat in his high chair.
He ate Pablum and strained fruit.

When his mother had marketing to do, Pig Pig insisted on being pushed in the stroller.

And at the market, Pig Pig would squeal and cry loudly until his mother bought him whatever it was that he wanted.

If his mother suggested that he fix his own supper because she was just too tired, Pig Pig would pout and say, “I can’t! I’m only a baby!”

Pig Pig's mother grew tired of it.

"You're a big pig now, Pig Pig," she said. "You've got to grow up."

But when she took away his old blanket and bought him a *real* bed, he sobbed like a baby all night long.

And when Pig Pig's mother packed away all of his baby clothes and gave him grown-up clothes, Pig Pig cried and cried.

"I want my baby clothes," he screamed. "I'm only a baby!"

So Pig Pig's mother gave in again, and nothing more was ever said about Pig Pig's growing up—until one day, on the way home from the market.

Pig Pig's mother had a very hard time pushing Pig Pig's stroller. It was full of Pig Pig and all the groceries it took to feed him. Up the hill they went. Slower and slower.

Pig Pig's mother puffed and grunted. She gave the stroller just one more push and collapsed!

The stroller stopped at the top of the hill. It hung there and then, slowly, it moved over the top and started to roll down the other side. Faster and faster it went.

"Momma!" squealed Pig Pig.
"My baby!" gasped
Pig Pig's mother.
Pig Pig kept squealing as the
stroller careened down the hill.

Then horror filled
Pig Pig's eyes. Below him,
directly in his path,
was a baby carriage with
a *real* baby in it!

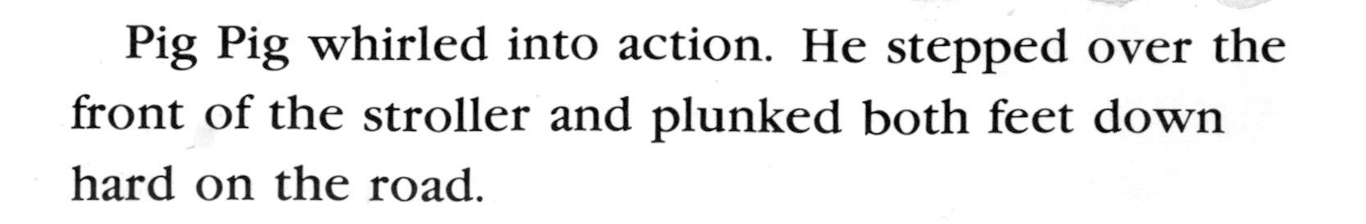

Pig Pig whirled into action. He stepped over the front of the stroller and plunked both feet down hard on the road.

In a cloud of dust, the stroller dragged to a stop just inches from the sleeping baby.

Pig Pig had stopped the stroller and saved the baby!

The baby's mother kissed Pig Pig on the head.
"How can I ever thank you enough?" she cried.
"Such a brave young pig."

By the time Pig Pig's mother had run down the hill, Pig Pig was surrounded by people. They patted him on the back, and shook his hand, and told him what a big brave pig he was.

Pig Pig beamed.

Pig Pig's mother hugged Pig Pig.

"I'm proud of you, my baby," she said. "You must be tired. Climb back into your stroller and let me push you home."

"No," said Pig Pig. "I'm not a baby anymore, and *you're* the one who must be tired. *You* get into the stroller, and I'll push *you* home."

And she did, and he did, and after that, Pig Pig was never a baby again.